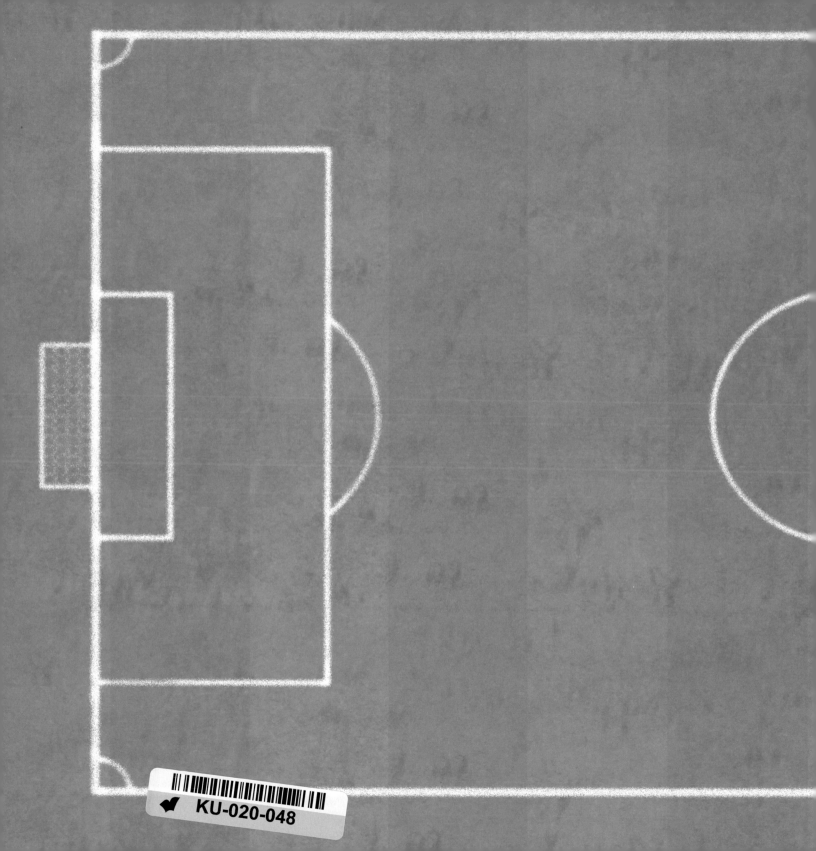
KU-020-048

Written by Gemma Cary
Illustrated by Tatio Viana
Designed by Sarah Allen

First published by Hometown World in 2015
Hometown World Ltd
7 Northumberland Buildings
Bath BA1 2JB

www.hometownworld.co.uk

Copyright © Hometown World Ltd 2015

ISBN 978-1-78553-029-6
All rights reserved
Printed in China

10 9 8 7 6 5 4 3 2 1

When I grow up, I'm going to play for ...

HULL CITY

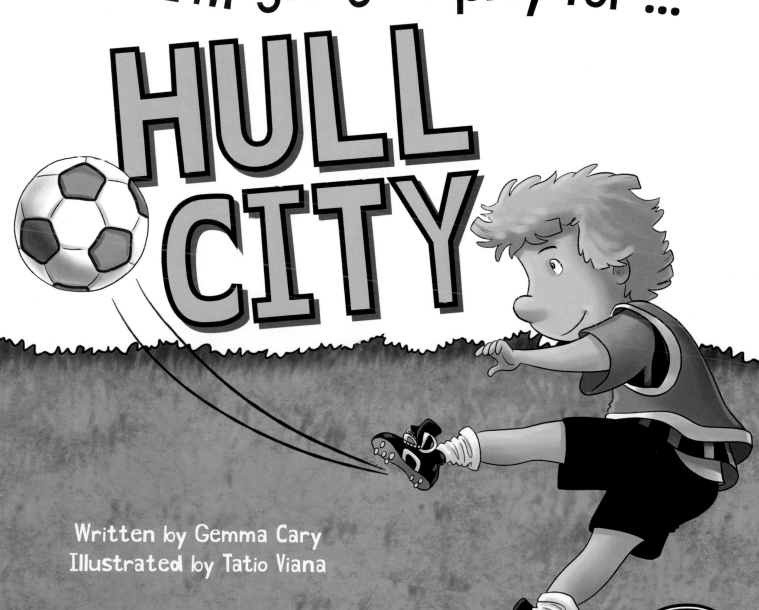

Written by Gemma Cary
Illustrated by Tatio Viana

CHILDHOOD DREAMS
HOMETOWN WORLD

"**Out you go,**"
said Mum, and the screen went black.

"**No!**" wailed Jack.

"**I was two-nil up!**"
"Very good," said Mum. "Now go
and play outside."
Jack glanced at the window and saw
their cat, Furball, scowling in the rain.
"**But ...**"

Soon Jack found himself outside, standing in a puddle. What was he meant to do out here? His football was flat and there was no one to play with.

On the back of his bedroom door, Jack found what he wanted: his
City shirt.

For some reason, he always felt more confident wearing this shirt, and he usually played better too. He put it on and instantly felt happier.

Back outside, it had stopped raining. Jack tossed a frizzy tennis ball into the air.

He bounced it on his knees and chest, doing keepie-uppies like his heroes from Hull City.

He dribbled the ball around the washing line, then sprang up and headed it through the air.

The ball sailed over the fence and hit something with a satisfying

thwack.

"Owww!"

squealed old Mrs Bettershed,
who had been busy digging up carrots.
"My bottom!"

Just then, Jack heard the familiar thump of a car door.

"Hello, Mrs Bettershed," called Jack's dad, appearing in the back garden. Mrs Bettershed glowered and speared the tennis ball with her hefty pitchfork. "Sorry," said Jack, trying not to laugh.

"Hello, Superstar!"

Dad held out a bag and Jack peered inside. It was a brand-new football! Not only that — it was in the colours of their favourite team, **Hull City.**

"**Cool!**" said Jack.
"We're celebrating," said Dad,
"because today is the first day
of the new season."

The pair were soon having their best-ever game of football. They seemed to play for hours!

When they eventually stopped for tea, Dad said, "I've spoken to our local team and they're having a trial tomorrow. They said you can come along, if you want to."

"Really?"
said Jack.
"Awesome!"

Next day, father and son arrived at the football grounds. The changing rooms bustled with children in blue and red bibs, nervously waiting to show off their skills.

The coach soon signalled for Jack to join a game and Jack raced over. He cheered when others scored and encouraged players who missed. When one boy fell over, Jack helped him up.

But secretly, Jack was worried about his own performance. When the half-time whistle blew, he had barely touched the ball, let alone scored.

Someone near the subs' bench caught Jack's eye. It was his dad, waving madly. Jack jogged over and his dad pulled the Hull City shirt from a rucksack.

"Wear this under your bib, Son. You always play brilliantly with this on."

Jack did as his dad said. As he sprinted back onto the pitch, he imagined he was stepping out of the tunnel at the KC Stadium. Amber-and-black banners rippled through the air while the crowd sang the team's anthem.

All of a sudden, Jack was the best player on the
pitch! In the second half he scored three incredible
goals, while no one else scored more than one.
He was confident. He was happy. He was ...

At the end of the trial, the coach called out the names of players who had made the final eleven:
"Danny, Olly, Leo ..."
Everyone clapped after each name.
"Joe, Sam, Joshua ..."

Jack stared at his feet. Maybe he hadn't made the team after all. "Freddie, Zac, Harry, Ben ..."

"Waaahoooo!"

Jack leaped into the air, waving his arms in excitement.

"I'll take that as a 'yes'," said the coach, and everyone laughed.

Dad couldn't stop grinning. He praised Jack all the way home. "You were amazing, Son! Unstoppable. A real champion!"

"Cheers, Dad," Jack replied. "I can't wait for my first match. But one day I suppose I won't be able to play for them any more."

"Oh? Why not?" asked Dad.

"Because when I grow up, I'm going to play for

Hull City!"

And guess who else is

going to play for

Hull City?

You are!

HULL CITY'S NEXT SUPERSTAR!

Write your name here

Stick your photo here

· ·

· ·

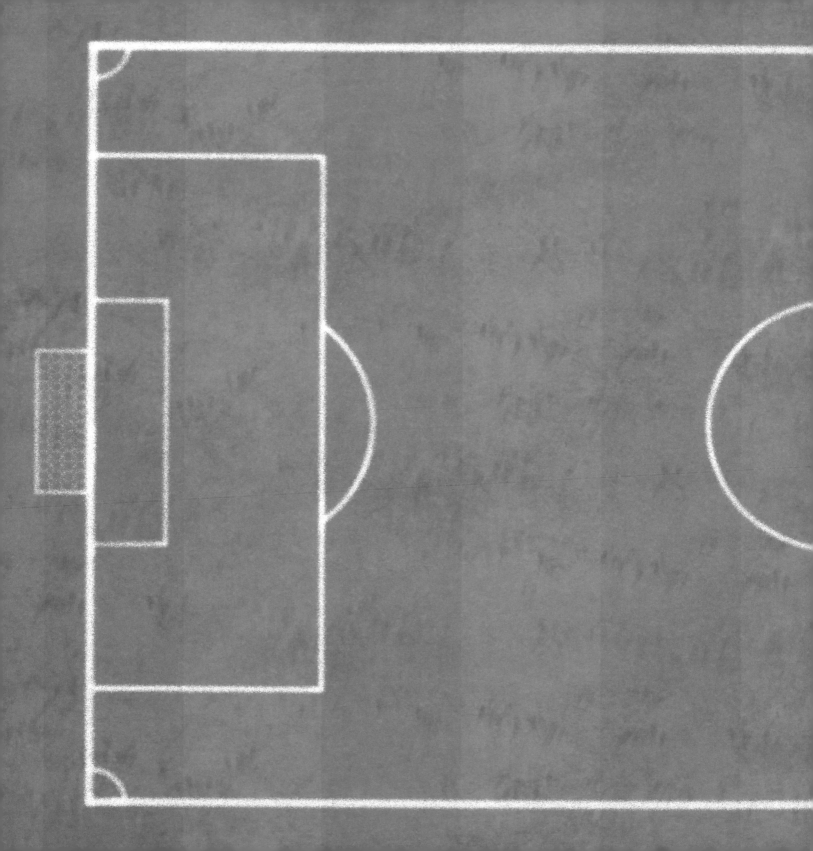